My Car by Byron Barton
Mi carro por Byron Barton

Translated from the English by Andrea Montejo

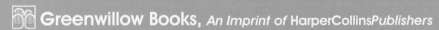 Greenwillow Books, *An Imprint of* HarperCollins*Publishers*

The full-color art was created in Adobe Photoshop™. The text type is Avant Garde Gothic. First Spanish-English bilingual edition published by Greenwillow Books in 2016
The Library of Congress has cataloged the Greenwillow English-language edition of this title as follows: Barton, Byron. My car / written and illustrated by Byron Barton. p   cm. "Greenwillow Books." Summary: Sam describes in loving detail his car and how he drives it. ISBN 978-0-06-245545-1 (bilingual hardback)—ISBN 978-0-06-245544-4 (bilingual pbk.) [1. Automobiles—Fiction.] I. Title. PZ7.B2848 My 2001 [E]—dc21 00-050334
16 17 18 19 20 SCP 10 9 8 7 6 5 4 3 2 1

I am Sam.
Yo soy Sam.

This is
my car.

Este es
mi carro.

I love my car.
Yo adoro mi carro.

I keep my car clean.
Yo limpio mi carro.

My car
needs oil

Mi carro
necesita
aceite

and a full tank of gasoline.

10.35

GAS

y un tanque lleno
de gasolina.

My car has many parts.

Mi carro tiene muchas partes.

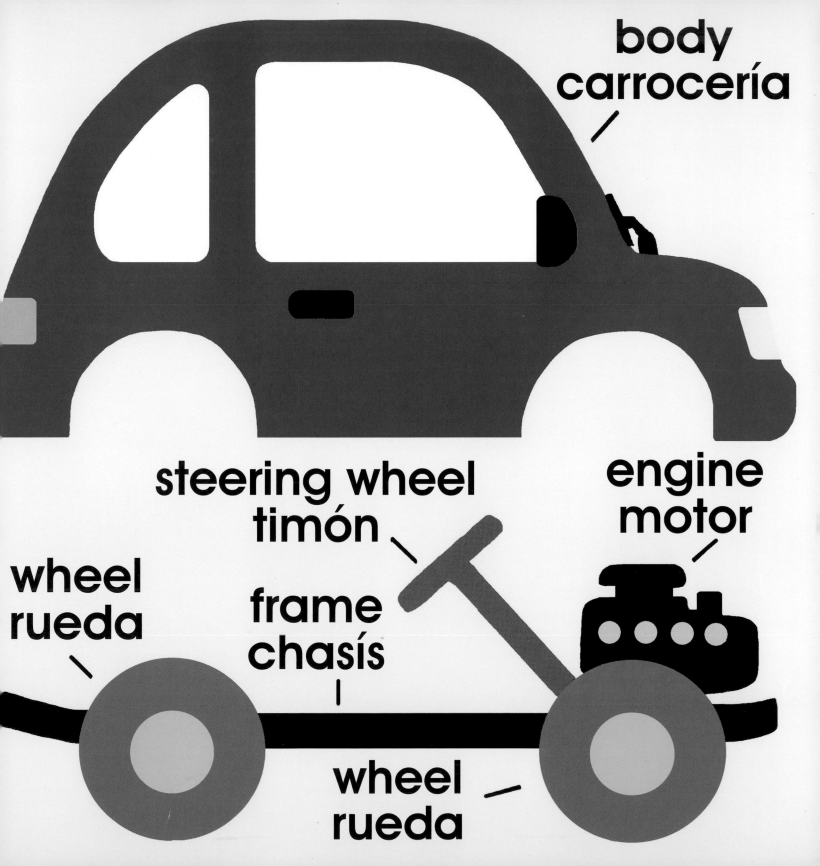

body
carrocería

steering wheel
timón

engine
motor

wheel
rueda

frame
chasís

wheel
rueda

My
car
has
lights
to
see
at
night

Mi
carro
tiene
luces
para
ver
de
noche

and windshield wipers to see in the rain.

When I drive,
I drive carefully.

Cuando conduzco, conduzco con cuidado.

I obey the laws.

Sigo las reglas.

Doy paso
los peatones.

SPEED
LIMIT
LÍMITE DE
VELOCIDAD
20

SLOW
DESPACIO

BUS • BUS

ONE WAY   UNA VÍA

NO
PARKING

PROHIBIDO
ESTACIONAR

I
read
the
signs.

Leo
las
señales.

I drive my car
to many places.

Yo conduzco
mi carro para ir
a muchos lugares.

I drive my car to work.

Yo conduzco mi carro para ir al trabajo.

But when I work,

Pero cuando trabajo

I drive my bus.

conduzco mi bus.

beep beep

5